Egyptian Mythology

Enchanting Tales of the Ancient World

Isaiah Covington

©Copyright 2022 by Cascade Publishing

All rights reserved.

It is not legal to reproduce, duplicate, or transmit any part of this document in either electronic means or in printed format. Recording of this publication is strictly prohibited.

Table of Contents

INTRODUCTION

Among the many views, beliefs, and mythologies of the world around, each has its own unique factors and manner in which they were observed. Of all these, however, the strong bond that the Egyptian culture had with the parallel mythologies and legends sets it apart as more intrinsic to everyday life.

While there were certainly fantastical elements to the stories and origins of the Egyptian people, the gap between god and man seemed to be smaller than in many surrounding cultures. The average man or woman in Egypt heard the tales since they were young about how the gods walked among the mortals; a side-by-side existence that permeated every part of life and society.

The pharaohs were not just empowered by the gods—they were gods themselves, and yet even that held onto a grounded foundation. The wondrous beings who created the world, and all that was around it trusted humanity to such a level that instead of simply *reigning over* what had been created, it became a joint mission of progress.

Where gods once ruled, the power of rule was then handed down within the immortal hierarchy until it was bestowed not onto some proxy for the gods, but to humanity itself. With the wisdom and strength of the pharaohs on the throne, the gods watching from skies, seas, and beyond, and the people living within that world all coexisting and growing from the connection, the thriving culture blossomed.

This is merely scratching the surface regarding the depth of Egyptian mythology, but the road you will take over the next several tales is a guide through life and death, creation and sorrow, and everything in between. Discover where the Egyptian world began, the beings that were there when it started, and pull back the curtain to see what was waiting for them once their mortal life ended.

This is wonder, power, myth, and life; this is mythology according to Egypt.

Chapter One:

The Egyptian Journey of Death to Life

When a citizen of Egypt died, rather than signaling an ending of a life, it was actually only one milestone that made of their existence. It wasn't only the manner in which you lived your life, but also the relationships you forged that would end up determining the direction your journey took following the death of the corporeal form. The beauty that was the line of life in Egypt is that it wasn't just a belief or hope, it was all-encompassing; family, friends, ethics, and religion—all played a role in the kind of experience one would have as they departed from the realm of the living.

For those living lives of luxury and wealth, hardly a thought was given to death-based worry, because with social and financial status came the peace of mind that you would be taken care of. For the average person, though, it was a lifetime in the making; every friendship and professional avenue was another step towards ensuring they would have a safe venture towards what was waiting on the other side.

This is the journey of one such average man who recently fell quite ill and then took a turn for the worse—here is the road his life after death took and how it all came about.

His name was *Ahmose*, although he wasn't sure if that mattered much anymore. Even if there were names in the Life After, surely with the number of the dead with the same name there would be some confusion.

Never wanting to step too far outside his comfortable space, *Ahmose* felt little at all when he glimpsed back over his life. Some happy moments, more unfortunate ones, but overall, nothing that would shift the label significantly towards a happy life or a disappointing one. It sort of just *was*, and so the indifference seemed fitting rather than bitter or a letdown.

He looked around and then back over each of his shoulders as the most recent of his memories—the posthumous ones—replayed themselves across whatever was acting as his mind. The uneven curtain over his doorway that he never got around to correcting had brushed the dusty floor when the last of the few mourners left the small room he had died in; that was his final living memory. After that, the fate of his ethereal life shifted from within his control to entirely in the hands of those he had chosen to trust.

The decision had not been an easy one, for as cautious as he had been in life, *Ahmose* never risked the chance that he would be lost to the nothingness after death. More of his friends than he would like to admit—actually, more like acquaintances—had died without putting forth any provisions for the necessary rituals to take place. Such a toss of the coin was not even close to worth it in his mind, and so well in advance, he made sure that what he did accumulate from a lifetime of holding back from *everything* went towards both the skill and care that would give him peace of mind.

None of this was ever on the minds of those in the upper class, at least not the *how* of it all. No one knew the exact truth about what they would encounter, but the guidelines were enough to lay out what was helpful and what was a hindrance. Leaving your dead corporeal body to the unpredictable factors of the environment meant that it wouldn't be long before the once-whole flesh turned to rot. Even in the commonly-dry, desert landscape that was most of the Egypt he knew, the decay *would* arrive and when it did the impact was much more widespread than just on the body itself.

That thought was a nightmare of the most terrifying kind for *Ahmose*, speaking literally as well as metaphorically. He would lie awake going over the details of his post-death preparation that the embalmers had explained, but even knowing the specifics did little to set his worries to the side instead of sleep and being able to relax during the windy evenings. He clung to the hope that his familiarity with the entire embalming process, and indeed on what would happen *afterward*, meant that whatever blind spots his knowledge had would surely fall within the purvey of the skilled embalmers. It was those craftsmen who made the ritual both an art and a final act of humanity and affection that brought *Ahmose* what little calm he was able to stitch together inside himself.

From the outside, it appeared to many as though *Ahmose* lived an existence that would call "boring" a wild definition, but what he lacked in experiences and luxury he more than made up for in the meticulous way he rationed everything in his life. Whether it was food, time, or valuables, he believed very strongly that if he dedicated *this* life to being responsible and even-keeled, then whatever was waiting for him on the other side was sure to be worthwhile. All of that started with the manner in which his earthly body was prepared for his journey into the Life After.

Once the soul ceases to be attached to its body and the bonds of life have been cut, the road to eternity begins. While the mortal world has countless opportunities to take shortcuts and skip over things of importance, the realm that awaits the soul does not abide by those who want to try and supersede the timeless process. It is for the soul to be judged, not for it to act above its station.

If nothing else, *Ahmose* knew that taking the time and resources to invest in the life that is waiting after death meant that when it finally happens, it will be without the fear of uncertainty. If the body is well-prepared for the embalming and mummification process, then it has a better chance of staying in that pristine condition throughout the soul's journey—which is not a simple one by any means.

The only benefit that is given to the dead is when they do make that initial transition from the realm of the living into the vast chasm of nothingness that separates life and death, it is not on the soul itself to navigate the treacherous waters that must be crossed to reach the true start of the Life After. It is shock enough for a soul to be dropped into nothing when they were alive, not seconds before, so if that same soul were to then be tasked with finding its own way to the Hall of Judgement, only the most skilled sailors and a few lucky ones would endure, but the rest would have been lost forever to the depths of darkness that stifle and suffocate the air between the two existences.

Ahmose was one of the thankful ones for this supernatural assistance in what could prove to be a challenging scenario indeed. He had often found himself wandering a street looking for some location and after *far* too long would realize that he was a quarter of a mile from where he thought he had been. With that kind of internal navigation, *Ahmose* found the idea that at least for a brief period—or however it was measured in the Life After—he would find the peace that frustrating optimists claimed waited for you after death.

Spending a lifetime being incredibly cognizant of every action, emotion, and decision became his routine and comfort zone, but that didn't mean it wasn't both difficult and draining. He would never admit this to anyone—living or dead—but there were more than a few times when *Ahmose* would envy a stranger who was doing something enjoyable that he just didn't have time for. Instead of the usual internal monologue about how that situation was proof of how his chosen life path was preferable to living on the fly, his reaction would be to wish that he could feel that freedom. Those times were fleeting, and he usually caught himself before the fantasies got too big for his buttoned-down mind. When they did happen, he couldn't deny that for a brief moment he felt happy just being close to the idea of a life without the restraints he placed upon both it and himself; finite happiness by proxy, you could say.

When it was all said and done—*literally* done—every responsible choice and missed social event added up to a dying man lying on a pallet with a soft smile on his face in the hours leading up to his passing. The mourners—seven in total, and most were family or others who felt obligated—would solemnly enter and then be met with the awkward situation of the one who was dying doing so with a smile, and the healthy mourner looking on with a frown so absolute that it might as well have been sewn on.

For some, it was simply the stark difference in *Ahmose's* attitude near the end in comparison to the common dying person, but one or two felt that same pang of jealousy that *Ahmose* had when he secretly envied those free spirits. Their faces, while determined to remain sorrowful, couldn't hide the struggle they were having with pretty much everything since they had walked over the threshold.

Of course, *Ahmose* was smiling; this is what he prepared for, and he couldn't wait! What he *didn't* count on was that in the final seconds of his life, when he expected the elation to reach its apex, something else happened; something that he did not like. Instead of his anticipation for the Life After rising and rising, it was like it hit a wall and dissipated into nothing, leaving a very different feeling in its place; terror. This particular *feeling* was unique because it came with a voice that used *Ahmose's* last moments to speak horrific words into his very core that resounded throughout every inch of his body and mind. Even as he sat now on the cold stone in the ethereal waiting-room-of-sorts, he couldn't shake the icy feeling that the voice had instilled.

"Why so joyful, oh damned one? Such glee. Such happiness. He sees nothing; knows nothing. All he feels is false, for beneath it hides what is real. Why do you hide it away from yourself? Is your guilt so strong that it controls your mind and actions? Shall you allow cowardice to keep its decaying fingers wrapped around your very self? Open your eyes! Open your mind! See what lurks underneath the ocean of denial you filled during all the years of naive existence!"

It was a cruel blindside. *Ahmose* didn't want to remember, and he longed for those first, blissful moments in this place where he knew nothing and every memory was a blank. The voice had its way with his mind, pulling back the curtain and exposing him to the fear that had been growing slowly within him. Despite every preparation and assurance, the journey that his soul would take involved more complexity than simply being ready would solve.

The embalmers had done their job and the coffin-maker truly put gentle care into the image of *Ahmose* that decorated its lid, but once that effort delivered him safely to the room he was now waiting in, everything to come was beyond what he could account for and expect.

The words that he had learned about within the *Book of the Dead* had been truer than even a deep believer like him had expected. *Ahmose* had ignored the naysayers that laughed at the constant efforts he made, but the foundation he built was all aimed at ensuring his death was only the beginning to a safe passage to whatever was waiting for him. Pharaohs lived every moment with the knowledge—unwavering and absolute—

that when their mortal form ceased to be, their voyage to the Life After would be quite different from even the most wealthy, influential man who was *not* a Pharaoh.

The average man, or truly anyone who did not rule over Egypt as the incarnation of a god, would be taken from their point of death through the chasm and barrier between the worlds and through the evils and unknowns that live and thrive on the edges of reality. The navigators always do their best to provide a safe voyage, but if the deceased did not take the steps to help *themselves*, it would be a rough journey with an uncertain ending.

For seventy days, the soul would venture across the many seas and expanses that were separating galaxies, lives, and thoughts. Each one of the seventy days would be fraught with danger, and the only way protection could occur was if the right preparations had been completed prior. Embalmed bodies remained in the same condition throughout the journey. The coffin shielded them from the sharp jaws and talons that reached out from the infinite darkness in an attempt to disrupt the journey of the dead. If the dead did what was necessary and those still living did the same, every attempt by even the fiercest of nether beasts would be harmless and unable to touch the soul being transported.

So it was that the soul of *Ahmose*, who had invested an entire life in preparing for the Life After, found a safe passage from life to death, and from death to the next phase of what was always waiting for him.

As he sat there, the remarkable stonework and craftmanship around him making the time—or "time"—pass without a hint of boredom, his eyes slowly widened as deep in his mind the whisper of that same cruel voice returned. Barely audible until he closed both eyes, focusing on nothing but whatever that awful *being* was whispering.

"So close. So close now. He thinks that peace remains, but it is fleeting and shall be nothing in time. Judgment waits. It has always craved for you, and now the road

ahead shall lead you to the inevitable end of a life of mediocrity. Now go, be judged, and let fire rage within your very being as the guilt already does. Fear; feel it writhing inside you. It is right. It knows best. This is the calm before the storm, and the downpour brings with it a doom eternal!"

Just as quickly as it had entered his mind, the voice was gone. He felt whatever this facsimile of breathing was, it was rapid and heavy as he tried to regain that sense of peace and calm back into his chest. The voice was right on time yet again, because as it had robbed *Ahmose* of those last few seconds in life, now it could not even offer him the peace that denial came with. Judgment did indeed wait for him ahead, and there was nothing more he could do to impact the result.

Suddenly, another voice spoke, this one outside his head and not disembodied with the desire to strike terror in his heart. *His heart!* That is what he had been hearing this entire time. It had been making him feel as though his life in this post-death place would be marred by the tortuous pounding that seemed to be underneath everything and everywhere he went from the moment he began this posthumous journey. He thought this ethereal version of his body was empty, but there it was, beating away as it had done in life; his heart was safely within his chest. The final piece that he needed to feel as though the embalmers had been true to their promises was now undeniable, considering he could feel the pulse—real or not—in veins that had felt stagnant until then.

He was ready; still struggling with the lingering fear, but *Ahmose* had done all he could. The rest was out of his hands and in those of beings he had only dreamt of seeing with his own "eyes". He *was* ready!

"Ahmose."

His skin prickled, or at least did its best impression of it; a voice had called to him. However, it was not in his mind, nor did it have an awful, malicious undertone. He had instinctively shut his "eyes" to avoid whatever was trying to scare him now, but something about this new voice made him feel safe instead of afraid, so against what his nature told him, his eyes opened.

He didn't know what he expected, but it certainly wasn't what he found standing about twenty feet away from him. In resplendent dress—golds, silvers, and jewels glistening and reveling in every ray of light—was *Anubis*, the guardian of the dead and companion throughout this journey. He watched to ensure the soul's passage to him was safe, and now it was time for him to lead this new soul to where *they* were waiting. This was something the jackal-god took quite seriously. There was genuine compassion for the gentler souls that found themselves in his presence, so the more comfort his presence was able to bring, the less fear they would carry with them into the place that they were to go next.

Ahmose didn't exactly know why, but without hesitation, he was standing, then walking over to *Anubis*. The god loomed over him, but not once did *Ahmose* feel in danger. In fact, something in those kind eyes let him know that everything the god could do to make this part of the journey smooth and peaceful would be made a reality. Granted, there was a moment coming up that even the power of *Anubis* had no impact upon.

Until then, though, *Ahmose* walked hand-in-hand with the gigantic, jackal-headed god out of the wondrously-built waiting area.

The only words that *Anubis* directed to him were when he called his name, but words were entirely unnecessary for the god to bring calm to the mind of *Ahmose*. Whenever the jackal god felt the soul begin to fret or worry, a single thought sent waves of contentment and all was well again. For some of the walks *Anubis* took with souls, it was a constant barrage of terror and anxiety that made even him strain as he found each and every bit of negativity and soothed them.

Ahmose, however, proved to not only be a low-maintenance soul to accompany, but even the silence between them radiated with positive energy. *Anubis* didn't expect this, and the smile that crept over his long face hadn't been seen for quite some time. Looking down at the small, average man walking beside him—the god's hands dwarfing the mortal—the god found himself rooting for this particular one. It wouldn't sway things one way or the other, but for the first time in a very, *very* long while, *Anubis* was hoping that this ended well.

Ahmose, feeling eyes on him, looked up and saw the jackal face smiling at him. Things kept going from unexpected to even more unexpected, but this situation only brought him peace. Even though he had no way to know for sure, something in his chest seemed to almost *purr* that somehow everything would be okay. He expected some kind of realistic perspective to jump in, but the peace remained, as did the belief that his life had not been in vain.

Then, with a sweeping hand motion, *Anubis* ushered *Ahmose* through a staggeringly large doorway and into the biggest hall he had ever seen or imagined; the Hall of Judgement. Stretching forever in every single direction, reality had no power over this space, and the way it seemed to purposely sprawl out and fill eternity with its presence was almost to spite the way reality ruled all else outside this realm. *Ahmose* had to stop trying to look around because the more he did the more his mind—even in its ethereal state—proved completely incapable of accepting and translating what his vision was taking in.

The sacred routines that he had only ever heard about were playing themselves out right in front of him. He stepped forward to acknowledge the forty-two *Assessors of Maat* who existed as representations of every sin that could be committed on the earth during one's life. Each stared at him in silence, hardly a difference from one to the next, but where *Ahmose* was sure he would feel the fear bubble back to the surface, only confidence made itself known.

The last step he took brought him to the center of the semi-circle that was comprised of numerous *Assessors*. With a deep breath—or what felt like one—he turned to the first in the curved line and began speaking in a loud, sure tone. As the sacred laws dictated, every soul had to speak out the name and purpose residing within each *Assessor*, then as they did so, admitting to the sins they *did not commit* during their lives. The *Assessors* who were spoken to without any admittance knew that the soul standing before them had indeed committed that very sin or not.

One by one he went through the line, each sin acknowledged, every word true, but he discovered the actual admitting part was *much* harder than he ever anticipated. It had always been this abstract situation that he had no concrete opinion on when he was alive, but now that it was happening to him, the mythical proportion didn't seem as enormous and overwhelming as it had before. The more he spoke, the more the confidence didn't just rise to the top, it erupted like a volcano of self-assurance. Not once did he cross into cocky or irritating, bringing a subtle smile back to the face of *Anubis* as *Ahmose* reached the final *Assessor*, nodding respectfully to the group as he began taking slow, backward steps until he was beside *Anubis* once more.

Placing a gentle-yet-giant hand upon his shoulder, *Anubis* looked down and gave his nod, though this one had the outline of sadness where only joy had been earlier. It must be time for the moment of truth in every way possible. He wanted to stand just as confidently as he did before the *Assessors*, but when the golden scales were brought out and placed in front of both him and the jackal god it hit him like a solid punch to the abdomen.

Reaching into a satchel hanging from his golden belt, *Anubis* produced a large, pure-white feather and held it aloft for all in the Hall to see. A low murmur swept through the space, everyone imagining the same thought in their own hushed tones; *The Feather of Truth* was ready to perform its duty. Within the seemingly innocuous *Feather*, was all the purity in the world. *Anubis* then reached out towards *Ahmose* with an open palm; it was time for the next necessity to be brought out as well.

The sensation alone was strange and almost sickening, so *Ahmose* felt immense gratitude that he was not alive to feel it; his heart began working its way out of his chest in a gradual, shifting motion until it fluttered through the air and landed with a wet sound in the waiting hand of *Anubis*.

Ahmose went to take a deep breath again, but the fear was back and it made anything besides short, sharp breaths impossible. With a *clink* of metal chains, the *Feather* was gently placed upon one side of the scale. The jackal god offered them a moment to settle before raising the still-beating heart of *Ahmose* into the air as he had done with the *Feather*, bringing the murmur to a full-blown buzz. With the entire place humming, nervous energy radiating like electricity, the moment arrived.

He wanted to look away, but if he knew anything, he knew that nothing he did *now* would do anything one way or another concerning the final judgment. Everything that was being measured now had already happened; all he could do was watch and wish that he still had the lungs to give a decent gasp or even a sigh, but still, the fear latched on tight. Then, as though the air was stolen from the bodies of everything in the Hall, silence fell. The only sound was the slow creaking of the scales as the heart was set onto the opposite side.

Up and down the two sides went, first the heart rising, then the *Feather*. Nothing seemed to give away the ending, and *Ahmose* had no clue how long this went on because it felt like he was spending fifty lifetimes staring at the golden scales without ever blinking—if he even had eyelids. In a muted, slow-motion, *Anubis* lifted his jackal head to stare directly at *Ahmose*; the god's expression giving away nothing about what the scales were about to reveal. He didn't even realize that the creaking had stopped and, with the slowest movement he had ever made,

Ahmose looked at the space between the *Feather* and the heart before letting his vision take in the entire picture.

In a burst of emphatic joy, the room went from silence to a full-throated roar of enthusiastic agreement. So often the judgment brought darker results, causing the entire Hall to bow their heads, but not today!

Anubis bent down and took *Ahmose's* hand in his before saying one phrase.

"Sekhet-Aaru."

The world around *Ahmose* split into nothing but brilliant white light. Everything was bathed in it, but he was now the only thing left. As the light began to envelop his entire form, the feeling that everything would be alright from now on permeated his ethereal body in one gentle surge of ecstasy. It had all been worth it; finally, it all meant something.

Almost as a balance to the way his life had ended, *Ahmose* spent those last moments before the light took over with a smile on his face. Nothing was wrong, nothing could ever be wrong again. Opening his eyes, he gave one last sigh and, still smiling, fell freely into the warmth of the illuminating world he had now been welcomed into.

Everything *was* okay, and *Ahmose* knew he could breathe in peace.

Chapter Two:

Atum and Nun – Before the Beginning

It looked like nothing; an eternal, shapeless, timeless space. This was *Nun*.

There was no land or air, no light, nothing to give any form to the dense darkness. Of course, it only *looked* like nothing. What *looks* like nothing but is in fact *something*? The answer to that was drifting beneath *Nun's* non-existent surface, just waiting and watching.

It had always been there in one way or another. Before it could remember, there must have been some existence, but in a place without time there was only ever the *now*. This was not how it always appeared, per se, but across an immeasurable span, it had grown and learned. What was once just a thought, became an idea, then that idea spawned others until it was an entire mind. Just because it seemed like nothing existed did not mean that it was the truth, for everything that ever would be or could be was lurking within that something of nothing.

Something was emerging.

The nothing seemed to shimmer for a moment, then another as if small waves were forming within *Nun*. In a plodding, shifting manner, there were lines and edges where no hint of shape existed before. The void moved and began to undulate back and forth, swaying within its home of darkness until one part began to slowly move apart from the other. Bit by bit the once-formless space became two distinct areas; one above and another below.

Neither had the sense of something complete, but the mind had been growing along with its surroundings. The knowledge that surrounded it poured into every cell as the once-thought began to form itself into something tangible and alive. Somewhere beyond what can be heard or felt, *Nun* was screaming as it felt itself tear in two. A haunting, practically soundless cry of pain, but it did not stop. As horrific as this was, creation is birth and *Nun* knew that the pain was the sacrifice needed for what was to come.

Nun was *nothing* no longer, for even though it was harsh and incomplete, there was a blurred sky floating above ink-black, choppy waters. Each wave seemed to do its best to reach the other half of itself—or at least what once was—and then it crashed back into the darkness to become one with its watery kin.

The space between the height of the sky and the water's surface was filled with a powerful energy that seemed to flow into and through everything. Each section of space and sea held a trembling, yearning potential for greatness and strength, then in the same breath, pain, and weakness. Every state and feeling ever to exist hung thick as the waves continued to reach and crash; this was the beginning.

Without time, there is no absolute way to know how long it took for all that power and energy to seek out the other. Where it was once spread out across every inch of existence, now it had converged into a single area, the waters churning violently as the meeting of the two sent waves and bursts out in ripples from the center. For a moment it seemed as though a whirlpool would open and the entirety of what had been formed—or what had made itself—would disappear and once again it would be—or seem like—a vast void of nothingness.

The noise was astronomically deafening, although that may have been because it was the first sound ever to be heard. Everything had been feeding into it, so this was simply the inevitable result of such power converging in one place. Such a ground-shaking *boom* turned the darkness into a blinding light for one fleeting moment, and then the waters calmed and the soundless atmosphere returned once again. It had all returned itself to a peaceful state, except for a massive rock that had risen from the water.

One would expect a rock that size, submerged for however long it had been there, would be a dredged up, slimy, moss-covered example of water decay. That, however, was far from the case. The surface of the rock was pristine and smooth, as though the most skilled sculptor had spent a lifetime smoothing it out. The rock towered above the shifting waters that it had risen from, now a stark contrast to the absolute black that had originally given it shape.

At first glance, that was all it seemed to be; a rock. Now, it was a *massive* rock at that, but even big rocks have quick limits to how interesting they can be. *This* was far from any rock that ever would exist, and not just because the pale color shone like a beaming star against the shadow-black surface of the sea as it lapped against its base. It had grown—or risen, or manifested itself—from the waters as a straight-edged stone, almost chiseled into perfect angles to form a square base atop and a tower that ran to the water's surface and below into the unseeing depths.

The stone had not gotten taller, but from all sides, it had begun a steady process of moving outward in a curved, forward-moving motion. All four sides seemed to follow the same pattern because it wasn't long before the cubic tower took the form of a just-as-gigantic stone mound.

Now, if that had been the most interesting thing about that event, it *still* would have been incredible, but it didn't stop there. Earlier it seemed as though the stone itself was shining, giving off some kind of illumination based on the polar opposites between the rock and the water. As the rock stopped shifting and growing, calm returned in a teasing, fleeting way. For a few moments, the charge of energy that had filled the air as the stone grew created a deafening pulse, then silence once more.

Just as soon as it had come, the silence was shattered by an ear-splitting *crack*. With the light from the powerful flash earlier faded away, the dim, murky view allowed for little to be seen. All was not this muted, blunted hue of shadow; atop the hill—the stone, which in its powerful birth was called *ben-ben*—lay a curled, still figure. From the skin of the man came steam and a soft hiss, sending glowing tendrils up into the air, lighting the hilltop with a soft, small area illuminated.

At the center of this ethereal glow lay the man, but he was no longer still. Arms and legs began to extend ever so slowly, as though they had never been used before. Every motion was intentional and also halted; the movements of someone testing out what they had never experienced before. In fact, that *is* what was happening; he wasn't just *new;* he was the first, but more than anything, he was a bit confused.

"What—I—hmm." The man spoke, but then gave a start at the sounds that came from his mouth. With wide eyes he moved his lips into different, contorted shapes, unsure of what had just happened. "Well, isn't this odd."

For all the knowledge and power that had gathered itself together for this man to find himself atop the *ben-ben*, speech was not something he was prepared for. After all, how could he have been? Granted, this was the result of every single piece of energy in existence converging and such a powerful event would never again occur, but that was then, and this was happening now. He had not always been this floundering figure on the top of a manifested hill of stone, it seemed like a brief second earlier he had been a swarm of thoughts, ideas, ambition, and energy. He didn't so much float through *Nun* as he existed and had done so since before anything ever was; he was not alone either.

The thoughts and ideas that had come together long ago to create minds and knowledge did not stop there. With a timeless passing, what had been minds gained desire and ambition, looking beyond the ever-dark surrounding that was *Nun*. Even that changed, though, for as these powerful essences continued to want and think of more, the entirety of *Nun* could not help but be impacted by the supernatural evolution that was occurring within it.

In the moments before the *ben-ben* broke through the black waters, *Nun* was buzzing and pulsing with a power desperate to escape. Every atom was anxiously waiting, and while they could not all lift themselves and find something more, when they came together it did indeed rise above *Nun* and what had been ambition was now a tangible, living, breathing man.

When he was in the depths of *Nun* with nothing but darkness to exist within, he was *Atum*, a mind of creativity and a deeper yearning for a purpose than anything else within its inky black. It never occurred to him that if he rose out of *Nun*, it would be an experience unlike anything he had ever known. In a timeless existence that stretched back further than even *Nun* could recall, finding something new was rare indeed.

Such a drastic and charged moment as the one that brought both then *ben-ben* and *Atum* from potential into reality was not without ripples and impact. That is to say that it is impossible for anything to be on one side of that surge of energy and move to the other without changing, and *Atum* had changed.

The entity which once desired and yearned, that had been known as *Atum*, sat upright on the top of the *ben-ben*—the mound which was still growing outward, slow as it was. Still perplexed and mesmerized by the movements of his brand-new mouth, he stopped and his face, which had just been amused and light, became a focused, furrowed set of features; something was different.

Atum knew the feeling that came from being pure potential, but this was not the same. In fact, it was as though the energy that had encapsulated his entire being was now swirling and stirring within him. Flexing his fingers out, splaying them to see what would happen, he couldn't ignore what was stubbornly sitting in his core, but he couldn't pinpoint what it was either.

"You're okay. What will be, will be," *Atum* said to himself, each word enunciated beyond itself thanks to the dramatic shapes he made his mouth perform. For those of us who have been speaking or around speech, it is a natural thing that becomes a regular, expected part of life; for *Atum*, it was not only new but foreign, even in this unspoiled shape.

Satisfied that he had tested out what needed to be, *Atum* began the long, shaky series of movements intended to get him from a sitting position to where he could make use of his new legs. It seemed much more efficient to survey what kind of world he had come into from his feet rather than seated with a straining neck struggling to glimpse the horizon. All his anticipation faded just as fast as it had arrived when he saw the world in which he had been granted passage. Somewhere deep in his mind, he assumed his eyes would fall upon luscious grass and forests lining the horizon, bluest skies gracing the air with the lightest wisps of cloud; that was quite far from the reality of his situation, though.

Nun may have birthed the *ben-ben* into existence, then further showed its power with the way *Atum* emerged from thin air atop the stone hill; it was still itself at the core. Where he hoped to find fields, he saw the same black that he had floated in for as long as his mind could go back. It was just as thick, just as visceral in texture. The ocean of inky darkness that stretched out in all directions was a sudden blow to his gut, sending a gush of hot breath from his mouth with a heavy tone of disappointment.

"But–no, this is where I came from." He felt his head grow heavy and his neck buckle as the hope′ dissipated. He began a slow, arduous descent from the apex of the *ben-ben* to the quasi-shoreline where the black sea met the pale stone. Kneeling, with the same effort and strain that all his new limbs needed, he stretched out a hand towards the uneasy waters. With closed eyes and whispered words to anything that might hear him, his fingers met the black ocean's surface and with a sorrowful shudder he pulled back to see the thick liquid dripping in large, congealed droplets, "Well," He said, cocking his head to one side as his mouth became a thin line of frustration, "I don't like this at all."

Time held no place within *Nun*, so as *Atum* once again sat atop the *ben-ben* he had no concept of how long it had been or even of the existence of time itself. The dark stains on his fingers were faded but still visible from when he had dared to reach back into what had once been his origin. Nothing ever changed—this he knew full well by now. Even the waves seemed to follow the same monotonous pattern as they rolled in, crashed, and then the current pulled the swell back out to begin the cycle all over again.

It could have been hours or weeks that he spent staring off into the distance with any glimmer of hope swiftly diminishing, the length of time wouldn't have mattered even if he could measure it. There were times when he felt the burning of boredom crawling deep into his mind as though it held a torch to the walls of his head. He had long tired of speaking aloud, for when the only chance for a response was from him as well, the point had ceased to make much sense to him.

When he stopped overthinking everything, there was a mild sense of calm, but that was asking quite a bit. It was not a matter of willpower or strength at all, because that would show *Atum* having full control over his body. Now, he was getting the hang of this new form little by little, but every time he felt sure that he had it figured out there would be an entirely new group of muscles that made themselves known, usually sending him back to the ground rather unceremoniously.

Existing as an ethereal entity allowed for knowledge to simply flow through and permeate his entire being during his time in *Nun*, but this was something entirely different. He would have a thought and then, seemingly independent from his conscious mind, it would branch out into twenty other thoughts, many completely unrelated to the one that originated the entire sequence. This increased his frustration well beyond what he felt when his arms or legs didn't do what he expected them to.

There were brief moments when he managed to get a handle on all of it, and as fleeting as they were, it allowed him the peace to feel what was at the core of his distress. Was he disappointed in his surroundings? Absolutely. Did the uneasy welcome in the human form make the entire situation more difficult? Without a doubt. These were not what ailed him, though, more like symptoms stemming from a deep, almost-hidden longing. This is what fueled all the other emotions and body-related difficulties he was experiencing; *Atum* was lonely.

It may sound simplistic, but when your entire existence was spent interconnected to something larger than yourself, it was a drastic and alienating occurrence to suddenly be on your own. The unplanned nature of the events that had happened within and around *Nun* meant that, as wondrous as the birth-like experience was for *Atum*, it had left him in a place of distance and isolation.

It drummed against every corner of his mind like a subtext beneath the other thoughts, taking a surface-level precedence. The only way it stopped tormenting his subconscious was when the other frustrations allowed for a brief distraction, but below the churning waters of his woeful, new existence sat that plain and simple truth; loneliness was devouring him from the inside out.

On one of the timeless stretches that he spent staring at nothing while hoping for *something*, a strange, blurred form caught the attention of his peripheral vision. He turned his head with a sharp, desperate jerk, not knowing what he might find but not caring. After so long with his own body being the only non-*Nun* movements around, this new distraction—whatever it was—gained every ounce of his focus. Just like when he first saw the bleakness of a world birthed from *Nun*, though, his short search ended in disappointment; nothing was there. Suddenly he caught another glimpse of it, but only for a second and it was just a flicker he caught out of the corner of his right eye.

"I know someone's there!" He kept turning around, his entire body rotating and then he began widening the circles, all to no avail, "Why are you hiding? If it's just us, come out and greet me. Why toy with me like this?"

The only response was the same silence that had hung in the dim air since he came into this phase of existence. He shut his eyes and hung his head. Of all the complexities that came with this corporeal shape, it was the exhaustion that always blindsided him. Eons of just *being* within the endless-and-without-origin depths of *Nun* had gone by without tiring, or so it might have been considering the lack of time itself.

For now, all he had to do was exist for a certain stretch of "time", although his boredom was delightfully bookended by this humanoid form giving out little by little. He never slept, for while he held a shape such as he did, the full weight of humanity had yet to come into being and so it was merely a step down in terms of endurance. One version of *Atum* had spent lifetimes upon generations in *Nun* without noticing a moment of it go by, but now the rules were different. He didn't like that; what he didn't like even more was that whatever was hiding from him continued to elude his sight.

However long it had been was never to be known, but his mind was starting to match his body in the impact this fruitless search was taking. The desire to seek whatever was hiding seemed lower than it had been, and while he still made the efforts to discover this elusive figure, it was at a much slower pace. With a gigantic sigh that seemed to take minutes to release from his lungs, *Atum* put his hands on his knees and tried to take back some kind of control over this confusing situation. This kind of focusing was usually done best with his eyes closed tight, but he couldn't shake the feeling that while he was doing that sightless focus work, there was something else there with him.

Wanting to take full advantage of the situation, he opened his eyes with a start and saw the strangest thing—certainly not what he expected. It is a popular understanding that an individual is less likely to recognize things in themselves than in others, and despite *Atum* being the first to tread this new realm of existence, that same truth remained unchanged. If *Atum* would have had some kind of enhanced awareness of his physical self, he would have seen something long ago that gave answers to the current questions he was asking himself.

In stark contrast to the surrounding ocean of black, there was a glow emanating from *Atum* as though his new flesh was illuminated. It wasn't the glow itself that had caught his attention, though, *that* was because of the dark silhouette which was staring right back at him despite the complete lack of any physical features.

Atum had found his shadow.

"What are you?" He reached out towards the shadow, unsure of what he was looking at. Pausing for a moment as he remembered the thick, dripping result that had come from his curiosity at the darkened shoreline, he finally let his fingers touch the ground and was both surprised and amused to find that there was nothing but the very rock he had stood on the entire time. It was not like the surface of water because his attempted intrusion hadn't caused a single ripple; in fact, he realized that the shape hadn't been disturbed at all at the location where he had made contact.

With a sigh that was more curiosity than the previous disappointing ones had been, *Atum* straightened back up into a fully upright stance, looking with a smile as the shadow followed his every movement without fail. When he raised his left arm, the silhouette did the same on its own side, then the same on the right. It didn't matter what shaking, jumping, or side-to-side shifts he did, his shadow was unfazed and still followed right along.

At every turn, *Atum* was unable to do anything that was not mirrored in a shadow-form on the ground in front of him, yet there was no hint of frustration within his heart. Instead, he felt that something had left him, but not in a negative way. It was then that *Atum*, staring with soft eyes at the shadow, realized that he wasn't alone anymore.

In many ways, the realization had more depth and meaning than he knew. The heavy weight of isolation had been sitting on his shoulders for quite some time, and it wasn't just the company that relieved him of that burden. The light that brought his shadow into existence wasn't from the sun that we all know, or a lamp or candle, nor from anything in the natural world; this was coming from somewhere real and true within *Atum*, winding through his new form and as it emerged into the air—thick as it was—it brought with it the gentle glow that was now gracing *Atum* with a companion. There was something about the beauty in the cycle; *Nun* had birthed the *ben-ben* and *Atum* into existence, and then from within *Atum* came the ability to meet his shadow at the moment he was feeling the most alone.

To the shadow, *Atum* was more than just the shape that it was meant to outline; this was its creator, and it loved him for that. *Atum* saw something more than a shadow before him, and with the same affection as his silhouette had for him, he felt love in his heart for what his illuminating glow had brought into the world. Everything has a path to follow and a plan that guides the road; this time it seemed like all the magic that swirled through *Nun* felt his loneliness and with compassion made way for this wondrous meeting.

In the world as it is now, the idea of a shadow is rarely one that is given attention or increased thought. Sunny summer days, grassy fields, and the varying shapes of the shadows as the day was experienced joyfully by all. *This*, however, is not the current world and the one that *Atum* existed in had been one of solitude until just a few moments ago.

To the fully human eye, nothing is distinguishing about a shadow aside from the size or length, and that is based on what is causing the shadow in the first place. For all the exhaustion, the boredom, and the loneliness, there was a great deal of *Atum* that was far from what one could call "only human". This is why when *Atum* looked at his shadow it was not one-sided; he saw a pair of striking, deep eyes staring right back at him. When he smiled, it was not directed at a slighter-darker area of the ground; there was a gentle smile being returned with the subtlest of dimples at the corners.

For all the wonder, magic, knowledge, and depth that existed within the inky waters of *Nun*, some things could not logically be determined or explained. No matter the breadth of power that *Nun* could use for creation, the concept of emotions tended to elude such straightforward thinking that encapsulated the nature of the minds beneath its dark surface. Therefore, *Atum* felt the hope so deeply, and the reason the pain of loneliness dug its talons as it did.

He had gone from an existence surrounded by thought and presence to a place void of anything save for himself, his new-found companion, and the inky waves crashing against the *ben-ben* from time to time. That had been jarring enough, although this particular moment was not what *Atum* would describe as "jarring" when he looked back in the later years. Was it unexpected and took him aback slightly? Without a doubt, but the place the memory held for *Atum* was inscribed with gentle affection and never failed to bring forth a smile. *This* was not a memory, though, for he was experiencing this sensation for the very first time. He didn't know exactly what filled his spirit so, but nothing to this point had come close to touching this part within him.

If his new corporeal form was a cavern, it wound into endless tunnels that wove for what seemed like an eternity. Some ended in walls, some in massive rooms with ceilings so high the light barely touched it, and some led to rooms that were so deeply hidden he had no clue what was in them. The first breath he took into these new lungs started his mind on a journey into the gaping mouth of the cave, and every moment since then had been a stumbling, blindly groping at walls, damp, dim trek that took both his conscious and subconscious—yet another confusing level to this new form of his—to depths that knowledge and mere information or fact cannot hope to reach.

Most of these previously unearthed areas held all the emotions that *Atum* had been trying to navigate, some with more ease than others as he found happiness a much simpler state to be in than when anxiety struck. To one degree or another, though, he felt he had done an exemplary job considering his complete lack of experience with any of this, but all he had come up against within his own mind was paltry compared to the two he was currently facing; loneliness and love.

"I don't–that is, I–hmm," *Atum* had been silently staring at his shadow for what felt like three eternities, and still he wanted to look at it for all the lifetimes he had left. At first, he worried that whatever affections had arisen were only there because of the terrible weight that loneliness had been placing upon him. There was a layer of truth in his fear, because the only thing worse than feeling alone was doing so when you had never felt it before. Was it enough to make him manifest something that wasn't actually there?

Taking a concern-laced breath, *Atum* closed his eyes and slowly let his lungs fill, and then with an exhale he did everything in his power to bring some semblance of stability to his senses. Knowing what to trust and what to wonder about was incredibly difficult at times, this time especially. He desperately wanted to open his eyes and find the shadow's beautiful stare still exists, but he also let himself drift to a place where his opened eyes found nothing at all. The pang of loneliness wasn't something he was used to, but it wasn't unfamiliar anymore, so when the pang suddenly grew into a searing ache, he was not ready for it in any manner.

Something hot and wet was burning in *Atum's* eyes, but when he went to wipe his eyes all he discovered was a clear, harmless liquid forcing itself out from behind his still-closed eyes. It was all culminating in a deafening cacophony of emotions, swelling to a crushing volume within his head as one thought sat center stage, casual and calm despite the destructive force raging all around it. Just when he thought the noise would cause his entire brain to ignite, he opened his eyes.

A sigh is, by definition, not a sound that would be considered loud or disruptive, but this one carried the entirety of *Atum's* relief within it and so what would have been just a sigh became a powerful sound that rippled outwards from the top of the *ben-ben* over the dark waters all the way to the edge of the horizon where the world fell into nothingness.

"You're still here," The tears were falling again, this time without any fight from *Atum*; he understood their purpose and what brought them into existence in the first place. Despite all the worry, all the empty negativity that had threatened his happiness behind those tightly shut eyes disappeared the moment he saw it was still right there, looking back into his glistening eyes, "I thought–I thought I was going to be alone again," He got the words out through stifled sobs, each one eliciting a longer pause than the one before as he struggled to find the emotional balance the situation called for. Although, in truth, he had no idea what to do at this moment.

With more of a natural effort than he had done before, *Atum* kneeled on the stone simply to be closer to his shadow—though it hardly seemed right to keep referring to it as *his* shadow, he thought. If *Atum* had the same understanding and concept of a shadow as we do, it would have been a dreadful insult to the object of his affections. This was not a result of blocked light or some science-based reason why it existed at all, because even the most intricate, scientific explanation would fall far short of what he saw when he gazed upon it.

Somehow, without uttering a single word, the shadow had let him know it understood and that they were in this together; two beings in a new, confusing, unspoiled-but-unprepared world. It was a connection that surpassed anything he had known, even including the time within the depths of *Nun*; this was strength and power and light and energy and wonder and terror and pain and laughter rolled into a mixture of ten thousand other feelings and senses. It was love—*Atum* was in love.

Whether one is an average, barely noticed human being from the modern world, or the first corporeal being ever to exist on this earth, there are apparently certain absolutes that cannot be impacted or changed. Nature is a powerful thing indeed, and the laws that are laid down within it supersede even the oldest, deepest magic there is.

This is why when *Atum* felt the love in his heart for the shadow before him, it was only the first spark and nature was more than willing to handle the rest. He wanted to touch the shadow, that much he knew. Kneeling beside it, or even when he stretched himself out on the ground next to it, was still not close enough. He swore he could feel a heat rising from the parts of the stone where the shadow touched, despite the usual cold sensation the ground gave off.

Holding a trembling hand just inches above the shadow, he took a sharp breath in as his fingers tingled as though a presence was lingering just beneath his touch. Nothing was even near what he was yearning for, and the more time he spent simply *looking* made him ache to have the shadow reach out as he did towards him.

He would close his eyes and imagine the dark fingers interlaced with his and from the burning desire sprung a bevy of curiosity. What would a shadow's touch feel like? Was it smooth or rough like sandstone? Could it speak to him, or are their minds able to link with others? With each question, he found himself clutching his fists tighter and tighter, unable to do anything but fall into the curiosity as if it was a refreshing pool; going deeper and deeper, each motion sending him through another current of questions—each one leading back to the same truth, the same reason that he was going through any of this; it wasn't enough. He may not have been able to verbalize what he wanted exactly, but he did know this; he craved for *more*.

Days that bring the best moments rarely announce themselves ahead of time; they prefer to wait quietly and enjoy the surprise and joy that comes from unexpected happiness. While there were no stars or moon to indicate the night, nor a sun to measure the daylight, he still felt the time passing in a muted, blunted-pain sort of way. He didn't want to appear ungrateful, considering that he was in a much better situation than he had been during those times of truly being alone, but that didn't mean he had to be perfectly content—because he was far from it.

He was continuing to do what he always did to pass the nonexistent time; gaze at the only thing in his world that brought him joy. Everything else was a bleak reminder that outside of this small haven atop the *benben*, it was a cold, desolate world. There were times when he thought he heard something, but in a nearly soundless environment, the rare noise he didn't recognize caught every bit of his attention that he had to give. It was never anything of value, usually a wave hitting a rock at a different angle than usual, or the sound of the choppy water lapping against itself; each time he would try not to let his hopes rise, but the same disappointment was waiting for him whenever he discovered the actual source of the "new" noise.

After what seemed like an eternity, his ears perked up less at the noises but he still gave a partial effort even though he knew what the result would be; a sigh of disappointment, a shrug, he would see the shadow follow his movement, and then his attention would be right back to the darkened-mirror of himself that stared at him with the same amount of love and content that he had seen the first moment they met.

Atum sat with his shoulders slightly hunched. He usually found some way to keep his spirits up by fully focusing on the shadow's eyes or drifting into the imaginary world where there was no earthly barrier separating him and the only other being in existence, but for some reason, he was only finding more sadness around each corner. Even the usual safe place he had built within his mind seemed to have lost its luster.

"There is so much I know," *Atum* began, his hand resting on the ground where the shadow's hand would be if it was not restrained beneath the rock of the *ben-ben*. Whether or not he was aware of it, during moments of heightened anxiety, his fingers would stroke the ground softly, some part of his mind allowing him the free moment to believe that he was actually holding the hand of another and not just hoping.

This time, though, he was convinced, "I used to believe that the waters of *Nun* had given me *infinite* knowledge; enough to navigate any realm or space with both ease and comfort. I've discovered quite a few different breeds of pain since this body and myself have been in each other's company, but the dull thud that is delivered when you realize you were only given a puzzle with half the pieces missing," He wiped a tear away, doing his best to fight off any others that threatened to spill forth; a battle he usually lost.

A deep breath brought relaxation to his jaw that had been tensed to stifle the possibility of future tears, then he continued with his glimmering eyes fixed on the gentle look that the shadow had, "How unfair—no, that's not the right word; not enough within it. It was almost…*cruel*," *Atum* trailed off, not showing that he was unsure of what to say next, but the weight of what he had just said out loud mixed with the inescapable truth of it sent his mind to its emotional knees, the realization swirling like a tornado both inside and outside of his head, "I have this absolute understanding of things that won't happen for more lifetimes than I can comprehend, and yet I was cast into this place with no hint of what the other half of that knowledge was to bring with it. Say what you will—no pun intended, my heart,"

He realized he was squeezing his hand into a fist as though the shadow's hand was going to be there for him to reassure. It only made him sink deeper into the melancholy that was fueling his current tone of speech, "Say what you will, but there is a sort of simplicity that comes from knowing some of what the future holds; the puzzle, for example. I know what one is and what it will be for the future, but I do not understand the way forward, nor was I told about the fear or pain or loneliness; especially loneliness. All I needed was something–*anything*– that would have prepared me for the isolation.

"You know that when you're actually *in* the waters of *Nun* things are quite…different. I was going to say that you can't see above the surface from underneath, but that's not right either. It's like your perception of everything is completely skewed; the way you feel, what you experience, *how* you experience. It is all connected and yet independent, but all existent within the same current. Then I get *here*." He couldn't help but give a sorrowful look all around, just in case his words had somehow influenced the atmosphere or lightened the thick black of the surrounding ocean, but it was all the same as it always had been.

The sigh that came next wasn't one he was expecting, as though it was simply a product of a timeless accumulation of emotional struggle, but he fully agreed with the sentiment, "It is truly the strangest thing, my love," His eyes welled up with tears that he didn't even try to stop this time, "I have never felt you, never heard you, and may never have more than this, and still, I find myself missing you. As though in some other place we were different and the world didn't try so hard to keep us on either side of this existence. If that is true, if there is some other version of us that found what we don't have, I wish them well and hope their lives are happier than ours by tenfold; perhaps then, when their cup overflows, some mercy shall fall upon us."

He didn't have the energy or desire to continue talking, so he slowly laid himself down and, with the tears having their way, did nothing but stare into the eyes of someone who was so very close and yet further away from him than anything in this world.

Down the sloped stone leading from the top of the *ben-ben*, over the uneven terrain as the hill became a rough, makeshift shoreline, lay the viscous, inky-black waters of *Nun*.

Ever since *Atum* had risen from its depths to be placed atop the *ben-ben*—which it also birthed into the new world—*Nun* had been there.

When *Atum* first laid eyes on the incomplete world he had been brought into, below the *ben-ben* watching it all, seeing the pain and the loneliness was *Nun*.

The moment *Atum's* godly glow revealed "his" shadow and all the wonder, confusion, and joy that came with it, the subsequent bond discovered between the two was all done within the all-seeing scope of *Nun*.

To the outside observer, this seems like a cruel, unfeeling act done by an emotionless, stunted thing that only existed to be a catalyst for all the life that would come after. It is not difficult to understand why one would come to those assumptions if the only information given were the situations that *Atum* experienced. That, however, is not the entire picture, or as *Atum* put it, you would only be seeing half of the puzzle.

Nun was always preset—always watching—but in parallel something else was going on; *Nun* was learning. There is an incredible gap between informational knowledge and emotional intelligence; while this may be a given for you, this was something that had to be *learned* by the colossal entity that was *Nun*. The belief that an infinite amount of time must relate to an infinite amount of knowledge is not only simplistic, it fails to take into account practically *anything* else besides the association between time and information.

Nun existing without a beginning or foreseeable end allowed for a brilliant accumulation of knowledge and from that came logic, then the ability to combine the two into a gargantuan, branching-in-all-directions understanding of where things were, where they would go next, and the resulting pathways from that point into eternity. All of that was floating around below in the thick waters, and as the timeless expanse continued, so did the growth of that information until everything that was, is, and will be existed within the thoughts of *Nun*.

As goes the tale of the beginning, this is how *Nun* evolved from nothingness to thoughts, ideas, minds, ambition, and then resulting in *Atum* perched on the top of the *ben-ben* waking to a new existence. In all that growth and expansion, there was not a single spark that allowed *Nun* to begin comprehending emotions. The logic explained whatever the brain or corporeal body was processing and doing, so anything beyond that was unnecessary—at least to the singular mind that was encapsulated within *Nun*.

The moments that led to *Atum's* birth—or rebirth, depending on the philosophy behind what *Nun* held as far as life—were as vital and explosively significant as they were anticlimactic. When logic and information are the prevailing factors behind a perspective, most situations could be considered "anticlimactic" simply because the response is being experienced without an emotional component. No fireworks, no cheering, no joy even, just discovery and a new understanding, or at least the beginning of one. The thing is that *Nun* didn't need to bring its effort together and produce the *ben-ben*, just as it didn't need to reform *Atum* and allow him passage into this new realm; it was something that *Nun* wanted. Without knowing how to define it, *Nun* was actually *feeling* something after the immeasurable passage of moment after moment.

It turns out that even for an entity that was fueled by logic, there reached a point where having every iota of information was merely a fact and nothing more. There was no more incline, no more discoveries; the numerous minds that had formed and grown through the power of pure knowledge were at a place that was never really considered because they were bored.

Now, that might sound like a rather insignificant problem, especially considering the terrific power and capability within *Nun*, but in this instance, it was not something small, but it was most definitely significant.

When *Atum* felt the full brunt of his isolation, it was so painful and traumatic not only because of the real struggle that comes from loneliness, but mainly because in *Nun* there was never anything close to "alone". Emotions, when experienced for the very first time, are some of the most powerful things that could ever be. They live outside knowledge and though one can read about them, without the experience it is only ever text without depth. *Nun* had existed without that level of depth right until that moment when it realized something that changed the course of everything that would come after; this wasn't enough for *Nun*.

So, from that desire for more came *Atum*; the representation of logic desiring to reach outside itself and grow into something else—something bigger. It was not only *Atum* who was learning about the impact emotions can have, the terrible ache that loneliness brings, or what it means and feels like to experience love in its purest form and then have it exist in a half-alive state; each time he struggled through something, *Nun* was watching and learning, but the more it observed and learned the more something else even more amazing began to happen; *Nun* began to feel.

It began as a slight blip, hardly noticeable but considering the complete lack of anything emotional, it radiated like a heat wave across the minds of *Nun*. Was this because of the intense desire to learn *everything* that *Nun* was beginning to change, or was it also because the being atop the *ben-ben* going through these struggles was still a part of *Nun*? Both factors made this something more than just another piece of information to absorb and understand.

What was another manner of discovery for *Nun* slowly evolved more of the emotional experience it observed in *Atum*. The ache in his heart sent the same slivers of pain coursing through *Nun*, every thought and mind enveloped by the overwhelming emotions being deeply felt by a man mourning the distance from his love. Some part of *Nun* that was clinging to its logical origins assumed that this, like many of the other emotions *Atum* had felt, would fade and lead to another, more in-depth understanding of this new kind of existence. However, as so many of us know, emotions rarely follow the path that logic lays out for them.

Just like the moment *Nun* realized its current existence was not enough—resulting in *Atum*—the feeling that something else must be done struck like lightning and residual sparks lit up the mind of *Nun*. Each one was sent down the sorrow-filled spiral that had been *Atum's* life from moment to moment, bringing with it a convoy of strange new emotions and feelings. All at once, the entirety of *Nun* didn't just want to understand and learn about what was happening to *Atum*, it wanted to do something about it.

"Please," *Atum* was still acting as though his hand touched that of the shadow, but no amount of hope or imagination could make him ignore the same cool, solid sensation of the stone's exterior. Even the perceived heat that he had thought was some indication of his love manifesting into something had faded, leaving him feeling more alone than even his usual lowest point, "Please, something *has* to change. I just can't–it's–just please, I don't even know if this matters at all. Why give me a voice if I am alone to use it? So, the echo that sometimes returns can give me a sense of comfort? That comfort left me the first day I saw what kind of isolation I had been plunged into, so *something must change!*"

He had fallen into distress before, even letting the tears flow freely, but this was the first time he felt the rage within him gather and rise through his body until it erupted in a violent, fully echoing roar. A noise of that magnitude had rarely been heard before and the echo alone carried his voice back and forth, almost from horizon to horizon, it seemed. No matter how distant the echo, the same pain could be felt in full each time. There was nothing about his experience in this world thus far that gave him hope to believe that his cry had found some merciful source, and so with the same mixture of sorrow and disappointment, *Atum* drooped his head and felt his shoulders sink as well.

While there was nothing and nobody above the surface of *Nun* for *Atum's* voice to find, the sheer power that was behind it sent the pained cry through the uneasy waters and into the realm and minds of *Nun*. It had been cultivating the desire to reach beyond itself and actually impact the experience of *Atum*, but with the limited emotional understanding that it still had, there was little direction to go on. Be it coincidence or destined, the voice of *Atum* rang loudly in the thoughts of everything within the void.

Were this to happen long before, the words would have been passed by without a single consideration. Again, this wouldn't have been because of any cruelty within Nun, just that the emotional component would have been far beyond reach at the time. As they were *now*, though, the depth of the emotions within the words that *Atum* had cried out meant that perhaps *this* was the moment that Nun had been pondering; the chance to reach beyond and to grow yet again.

Atum hadn't looked up from the tear-blurred ground for quite some time. It all felt too much for him to take in and the more he thought about it, the more anger he felt burning. None of this was of his choosing, and with so much of it out of his control, it seemed like a malicious game to have him alone and then teased with a literal shadow of a partner in this somewhat life.

His ears picked up an unfamiliar sound, but after countless disappointments, *Atum* wasn't too keen on doubling up on being let down. With a deep sigh and a resolve to sink deeper into this darker plane of emotions, he continued his mindless staring. That is when he heard something he *definitely* didn't recognize or expect.

"*Atum?*"

His head jerked up so fast he was sure that it was going to fly off his neck and into the dark sky. It took a moment for his vision to clear, considering the waterfall of tears that had just recently came to a halt. There, standing right before him, was the shadow.

He tried to both stand and fall back in shock at the same time, causing an awkward half-stumble forward, but eventually, he made it to his feet successfully, only to be struck dumb again as he realized who he was looking at. The shadow was just staring at him, its kind eyes now even more brilliant outside the transparent walls the stone had it caged in.

"I don't–how?" It was all he could manage to spit out. There were hundreds of fully formed sentences he wanted to say, but considering the jumble going on between his mind and his mouth, getting any words out at all was quite the accomplishment. It didn't seem like the shadow was having any trouble understanding what he meant—a benefit of spending a timeless amount with someone, even in silence. There was an unspoken energy between them; something powerful and magnetic that transcended barriers and the need for anything besides the other.

"I don't know," it whispered slowly, each word a new experience, "First I was there," A blurred, dark finger pointed to the stone where it had been only moments before, "But then I wasn't there. I don't remember doing it, but I *do* remember asking for it so many times. Did you summon me?"

This immediately welcomed a sweeping grin to *Atum's* face, any of the negativity from earlier had been washed away by the presence of the one being who understood him. He never considered that for all the times he begged and asked for the shadow to become as real as he was, beneath the harsh rock was an entity in love doing the very same thing; asking to be freed.

"You know what," He chuckled, every muscle in his body feeling more at ease than they had since he first appeared atop the *ben-ben*, "I don't remember doing it either. You don't think–" *Atum* turned to look at the black waters, but as far as he could tell there was nothing different about the waves; same surface, same thickness, and yet there was some small part of his mind that knew a change had occurred.

"I don't care how it happened."

"Neither do I."

The shadow felt even more comforting and gentle than he ever could have imagined. His hand rested softly on its face. The stark contrast of his skin to the dark blur only made it even more beautiful to him. They both felt the rush of heat in the air between them, and then their lips met.

So it was that the first god of the world, *Atum*, found love and companionship with the shadow that had once been simply "his". From the power of such a union came the births of two new beings.

First, emerging from the mouth of *Atum* like a humid, heavy breeze, came *Tefnut*, the emblem and god of humid, corrosive air that encourages change, creating the concept of time. After *Tefnut*, a second deity also began to spill from *Atum's* mouth, this time in the form of a cloud. The goddess *Shu*, a symbolization of dry air and the force of preservation.

Atum looked around him and saw that not only was he no longer alone, he was standing on the same *ben-ben* that he had been when this all began but now, he was surrounded by more than just the black ocean; he was surrounded by family.

Chapter Three:

Creation and Destruction

The world was still new and while the dark, thick waters of *Nun* continued to churn and cover all save for the *ben-ben*, change had broken through. The two offspring of *Atum* and the shadow, *Tefnut,* and *Shu,* discovered that their power was greater than even they knew in the early days after they came into being.

Shu found joy and distraction by circling the air above the *ben-ben* and slowly, little by little, the darkness and heavy nature made way for what turned out to be a bright blue sky. Still, her father worried about her without end, so the only place where the sky was clear and free was above the only home she ever knew and feared that she ever would know.

Tefnut was just as adventurous but never seemed to test his father's boundaries regarding the *ben-ben.* As his sister created a pristine sky above them, he followed right after and where he flew there appeared moisture that began banding together the more *Shu* circled the path her brother made. It wasn't long before the usual depressing sky that *Atum* had known for hundreds of lifetimes was replaced by a cobalt blue with wisps of white clouds here and there. His children had not just randomly created, there was a silent art that embodied the entirety of all they had achieved.

After living with the emotions that came from the life above *Nun*, *Atum* was becoming more and more adept at navigating the more unexpected of them. One that he was adamant about pushing down and ignoring was when his children displayed the true scope of their abilities because a whisper of a voice within him knew they needed more freedom than the *ben-ben* provided. Every single time this thought popped up, he would do everything possible to strike it down, and it usually worked, but for some reason, this time… it was lingering.

"They really are good at that, aren't they?" *Atum* hadn't even noticed the shadow behind him, but the voice did nothing but bring him comfort so he simply smiled and nodded, leaning his head back onto its blurred shoulder.

"Yes, *here* they are, but you know very well I can't see past the horizon. What if that is not where it ends? What if the drop is further on and there exists an entire place I cannot watch over them?"

"My dear, they—"

"I'm being overprotective, I know." He didn't even realize he had cut the shadow off, but with compassion, his love just nodded and let him continue on. He usually talked himself back to the right place, and this just seemed like one of those times, "I was alone for so long—you know—and so every time I think about them taking flight on their own and setting off to make the rest of the world pristine and clear, I only imagine them never returning home.

"You and I were allowed to find each other, but what kind of situation surrounds that miracle? I will never know the true span of lifetimes that I sat alone, right here where we are now! I looked up into *that very sky* and do you know what I saw," If it were to answer him, it wouldn't really matter because it wasn't actually a pause with the intent for someone else to answer; he was pausing to gear up for whatever branches of thought his mind was steering towards at the moment. His shadow could tell that this particular moment was going to be a troublesome one for her love, because if there was one thing that he feared more than anything it was being alone again, "I saw the same thing, no matter when I looked or how often I did; darkness. The longer I looked, the more I felt it in my core. It may sound selfish or perhaps it actually *is* selfish, but when I think of all I went through to get here, to be with you and to have them,"

He pointed to where *Shu* and *Tefnut* were laughing as one would soar through a cloud and then the other would repair it before repeating the game all over again, "Just look at them. Absolutely perfect in every way, and I am just supposed to let such amazing, pure beings disappear into the volatile world without a fight? I can't see the purpose in that, nor do I see myself simply standing here while their forms get smaller and smaller in the distance."

"Well," The pause was different this time, and the moment for someone else in the conversation had arrived. The shadow knew that Atum was fighting with himself. This had very little to do with what it thought or having another perspective on the matter. The person speaking now was talking directly to the voice deep within *Atum* that was quietly letting him know it was time to let his children pave their own way. "What do you propose we do, then?" She had done this dance before, and actually, this particular one was a favorite of theirs. The timeless passage of moments meant that forever and now had little difference, but the way each of us perceives that passage dictates what time actually means to us.

"I mean–" But this was the part where she knew the direction that this needed to go, and if she just let him cycle through the variety of reasons, he would end up back at the beginning and they would go through the isolation of his origins in this world all over again. The shadow loved him beyond everything, but part of that meant knowing when she was better for him than he was.

"I am sure the children would be perfectly happy living the same kind of life that you did." The shadow paused and readied for the expected response.

"Same kind of life," His tone became high-pitched, as it always did when she was right and he desperately did not want to admit it, "I was–"

"Alone, yes, you were, but stop thinking of it in the *exact same* parameters, my dear," She knew that he would soften just a bit at her gentle tone. It may have appeared like a game, but this was not a playful thing to her. You don't spend several eternities alone, and then another at an arm's length from the only other being in existence, without some trauma and pain lingering all around and within him. She knew this from the pained energy he radiated when he thought one of the children was flying too high or dared to descend beneath *ben-ben* to observe the inky waters, or the depth of his worry when he fell into a truly dark place that even she struggled to pull him from. Thankfully, this was not one of those hopeless moments, but she still understood and loved him enough to not manipulate, but *help* him get to where a wonderful part of him knew he should be already.

The first time this had come up was when *Tefnut* first realized that gravity had no control over his form, and with a little concentration and effort, he could soar through the air as if he weighed nothing at all. His sister was wide-eyed and jealous, arms folded over her chest with the best pout she could muster, as she followed his patterns with her head despite trying to look uninterested and unphased.

In a world without substance, noise is something of a random event that can depend on far too many factors to try and guess the result. Sometimes the screams of the children playing would race to the edge of where the *ben-ben* stood and then it was as though the sound became muffled and dropped, but other times a simple laugh would bounce back and forth as an echo for what seemed like far too long for it to be common.

Both *Shu* and *Tefnut* found it hilarious each time and jumped up and down to see if the height of the noise affected the echo or not. While that experiment didn't produce any viable results other than fun, it did succeed in showing their father the impact stress can introduce. The shadow recalled how both children stood there, stone-faced and silent after *Atum's* voice won the echo contest without question; his prize was yet another reason to worry about his children. It had taken the shadow forever to convince him that children jumping would not impact the structural integrity of the rock they currently lived on.

"You are being far too literal when it comes to your children's experience in comparison to yours," the shadow brought him back with gentle words while also reminding that little voice inside him needed to help her out here. It was a difficult enough path to navigate when he was dead set on being the overprotective god-of-a-father, when that whisper of a voice got too exhausted to shout down the others it was a bit one-sided. They had come so far together since those moments, though, and every day it saw more and more growth from the man that had stared back for all that time, per se, "Yes, you were alone, isolated for longer than any cognizant being should be, especially after the community within *Nun*, but set that aside for the moment, please, *Atum*,"

His name was reserved for the times that it wasn't just the direction but also the tone that needed clarified. Shadow was serious about this matter, even if it inserted some frivolity into their back and forths, and by letting him know that in a compassionate, gentle way they could avoid a distance in approach, causing a gap in communication. The shadow, while not a god, still radiated with brilliance despite what the blurry, silhouette form might indicate; there was no dimness in its mind, for it had originated as the reflection of a god.

Even though neither of them knew the absolute truth, the shadow was sure that a large part of the bond that brought them together in the first place was because of the love they shared. Love in itself can be one of the most powerful things ever to exist, but when something first enters the world, it does so with such purity that nothing can ever match that initial burst of creation and manifestation; this is why the shadow knew that their love was capable of accomplishing anything set before them. Working through the ups and downs of parenting was certainly within those parameters.

"Okay, so I'm setting aside the specifics to see why their situation and mine are similar?"

"That's what I would suggest, at least." She did her best to hide the massive smile that wanted to break through. Something inside him was embracing the idea of this kind of change, and that was temperamental territory indeed.

"Because I was stuck in the same place without an end in sight, and I felt like I had practically no control over anything," the shadow nodded as he spoke, the elation within her heart making her feel like her body was bouncing up and down despite the motionless stance she remained in, "Even though I know that I felt truly alone, that doesn't mean that they won't eventually feel the same—or close to it—by being caged in, even by family."

"I couldn't have said it better myself," And there was no hint of platitude or sarcasm in her voice, only pride. The shadow watched in wondrous awe as *Atum* worked through the situation, his pain and trauma battling against the part of himself that wanted his children to have *better* than he did, even if that meant finding some peace at the prospect of letting them go.

"What if they don't come back?"

"You've seen them grow and learn," A gentle, shadowy hand rested on *Atum's* face, drawing a contented sigh from him as it continued, "I don't think it's an exaggeration to say that those two," They both looked up at the children, still soaring around without a care in the world, though this time they were making rows of cloud shapes for the other to fly through, "Can do anything, wouldn't you agree?"

"I couldn't have said it better myself," He said, chuckling at the smirk that was thrown back at him. He pulled her close, never growing tired of the feeling he received when his arms were holding his dearest.

"Well, then—" pausing to kiss him, "I would think that *anything* is a pretty good measurement of whether they are ready. I mean, if something out there is more than *anything*, I'm sure we'll hear about it."

"You never know, dear," He looked over his shoulder to where the skies still matched the pitch-black depths of *Nun* below, "In this world, I don't think the rules end at *anything*."

It took several more conversations that were similar to the one that the shadow had hoped was the "breakthrough" discussion, but, as he always did, eventually, *Atum* realized that as wondrous as the place had become for him, the *ben-ben* was swiftly becoming a prison for his children. Instead of the endless flying and games, they both spent more and more time by the water's edge or hovering at the closest point to the appointed barrier, eyes set squarely on the horizon. It was time to let them explore the world for themselves.

"You'll see, father," *Shu* said as she embraced him, "We'll make everything, better."

"Oh," Tucking a stray hair behind her ear as he did his best to hold back the inevitable tears, "Of that, I have no doubt at all. Between the two of you," He pulled her brother close as well, looking at both of them as he spoke, "There is not one thing out there that you both cannot achieve, and if anything stands in your way then rely on each other to emerge on the other side safe and sound."

She had never seen her father like this, and while *Shu* knew that it was tearing him apart inside, it was just as hard for her to admit to herself that it was time to adventure outside of her comfort zone. If it had just been her venturing out into the world her confidence would not be at the level it was, but anytime she felt the pang of worry all she had to do was look to her side and there was *Tefnut*, ready to be there beside her for anything and everything.

They had talked about it for longer than she could remember, *Shu* and her brother. The idea of venturing out to see what else the world had to offer had been a curiosity since they first flew high into the air above the *ben-ben* and saw the expanse that *Nun* covered in all directions. To their father, it was doom and assured destruction, but to the two of them, it was a world filled with potential. Incredible things were possible, and with the power of their father flowing in their veins, and the brilliance of their mother fueling their minds, potential was just another word that meant waiting for them to bring the change.

Shu heard *Tefnut* speaking to her father and mother as she turned to look out at the dark waters. How many times had she been in this exact place, looking out at the same ocean and darkened skies, hoping beyond hope that she would one day leave to explore and improve the diminished light she saw all around her? There were moments she never thought this would arrive, that her entire lifetime—however long that stretch of eternities would go for, she didn't know—would be spent in the same place her father had called a torturous place.

For a time, she could alleviate those feelings by jetting off into the skies to find even a tiny section that was not as clear as it could be, but even that became futile after the hundredth time she found nothing but the same thoughts of being stuck.

For all these internal struggles and feelings, *Shu* knew that whatever was unfolding in her brother's mind was far more intense. He was naturally the more intense of the two, but he also excelled at controlling his emotions and repurposing any negativity into some kind of productive action. The more times that they both realized the entirety of their sky was pristine, she began to notice that his usual calm demeanor was showing some cracks at the seams. He was strong—he had to be to maintain himself with the torrent of emotions that endlessly coursed through him—but everything has a breaking point, and she never wished for him to reach his.

That is why, as she turned back to see her mother hugging *Tefnut* tight, a genuine, earned smile crept from one side of her mouth to the other.

"What are you smiling so big at?"

"The possibility of flying away from you the first chance I get." She laughed and leaped forward at her brother, who was matching her smile inch for inch. They both let themselves feel the incredible joy of the moment because it was always a hope and never a promise. Today everything changed for the better, and that is exactly what they planned to bring into the world that was waiting for them.

The shadow walked over to her dearest *Atum* who was doing his best to act natural, but his tense shoulders and nervous fingers gave him away. Considering what was about to happen, this was incredible for him but she knew that there would be some point where the calm exterior would give way to the mourning father underneath, now whether that would be before or after they left, she didn't know. She also wasn't sure which was preferred, although if she set any selfish intent aside the best situation would be for him to send them off with a smile and his blessing, then as they disappeared into the distance and the reality landed he could break down without risking any impact on the children's journey.

"They're going to come back," She quietly mentioned, holding his hand, "Give them the send-off they deserve, because of all things *that* really is within your control."

He smiled. The shadow was always right, especially about matters such as this. There would be time for grief, and he was certain that it would be excessive and dramatic, but for now, he would be the strength his children needed to fly into the unknown world with confidence. It was not for the mere sake of it that they were venturing out, the world needed them and without them there was little chance for things to improve.

It made sense to him now, even if it still hurt; because he had experienced the gift of a world that was better now than when he entered it, his children could find that same wonder if he was willing to offer them the independence that had been thrust upon him. Someday when they returned to him, it would be with a better world in tow, and for that he was exceedingly proud.

The shadow was so proud of him. For every moment that arose for *Atum* to take back his blessing or collapse into tears, he instead put forth a composed, proud energy until the moment the small dots that were his children disappeared over the horizon. Within an instant, he let every single wall tumble down and for the first time since he made the decision, *Atum* suffered. In his chest and head, in his soul, through his veins; the ache of the two empty spaces before him dug into his entire being like hundreds of talons gripping for dear life. The shadow had expected something of this extent, but the degree with which he broke down was far beyond anything she had prepared for.

Horrible, wrenching howls poured forth from him in between the sobs. The shadow didn't even attempt to console him because anything she said—or tried to say—was lost in the haze of tears and gasping breaths. He would reach up from time to time, pointing to where the children had flown off from, then fall right back to the awful sounds that orbited the crying. It would pass, this shadow knew, but until it did there was no place else she would rather be than right next to her *Atum*.

He would fall asleep, giving a shudder every now and then with a small cry, but for the most part it was peaceful. There were certainly times when she had felt like the odd one out in her own family, but not because of a lack of love on any front, it was because she couldn't help but compare to the other three and in that light, its lack of power created a lack of confidence as well.

This was not a new fear, it was something that had haunted her since the first few moments after she had been granted complete existence, free from the stone of the *ben-ben*. The shadow knew why she adored *Atum*; he was immense in character and integrity, devoted as a partner and a father, but more than anything it was because of his true power—which was surely mighty above all else—remained dormant below his surface. Whether he preferred to be a more corporeal version of himself or the depth of his power was frightening even to him, she didn't know, but what she *did know* was that the strength of self it took to control power rather than unleash it was worthy of admiration.

In truth, there could have been lifetimes of love between them even if the only reason was the miracle of the shadow emerging into existence, but with the foundation of genuine affection beneath them there was no limit.

So, she sat there, arms around the sobbing *Atum*, feeling nothing but love and gratitude for the existence it never thought could be possible.

It didn't take very long for *Atum* to begin pacing back and forth along the final point where *Shu* and *Tefnut* had flown away from. It was a common area along the cliffside that fell down a sheer drop to the inky black below, but when *Atum* looked around, he saw illuminated footprints indicating the last few paces taken by his children before they soared off. Every thought was underscored by this little voice reminding him that they were making the gloom-ridden world a better place, and for that, he should be delighted.

This was not taken well, since *Atum* was well aware of the positive motives for his children's endeavor, but didn't *wish* to be logical at this moment. He had been calm throughout the farewells and as they became smaller and smaller figures in the sky; he had earned the right to set aside logic and understanding instead of simply giving in to the grief of a father who didn't want his children to leave the home they all knew.

His shadow had known that *Atum* would resort to pacing fairly soon after, and right on schedule, he was at that spot staring off before going back and forth again. She would give him a while before trying to soothe or comfort him, so for now she was content to sit back and make sure he didn't try anything drastic like leaping to see if he too could fly— which he couldn't. Soon enough the children would appear on the horizon and this entire ordeal would be forgotten and replaced with his overwhelming joy at seeing his beloved offspring once again.

"Just be patient and trust them," She said to herself, keeping both eyes on *Atum* as he was peering over the edge. It was fitting that he couldn't fly, because every time he got too close to the sides of the *ben-ben's* flat top he started sweating and backing up until he felt safe enough to breathe fully again. It wouldn't be his own idea to go tumbling off the side, but mixing grief with balance rarely goes well, and so she continued to keep a close watch, "Soon now."

It was not soon, in fact, it had stretched far past soon and was entering a territory where even the shadow was joining in on the pacing without any attempts to calm anyone. Of course, this didn't help *Atum* who was hoping that his steadfast love would rein him in, but for her to be showing this level of worry sent his mind into a frenzy.

"You said soon," *Atum* said, not wanting to sound angry but knowing he did anyway. They weren't pacing in sync anymore, now it was an awkward passing of each other every now and then, always in silence. It was too much for him. Being outwardly sturdy was not something he was used to during times of emotional struggle, because the shadow had always been right there for him to lean on. Now they were trying to lean on each other, but the new dynamic was certainly having its growing pains right out of the gate.

"I thought it would be soon," She retorted, purposely adding a huff to her voice, "Do you think I would say soon even though I thought they would be gone for *this long?*"

He couldn't remember the last time he heard his shadow raise her voice, the gentle touch was usually the approach taken, but this time he was the offender and she was offending right back. There was no reprieve from the constant worry, save for the moments of terror where one or both of them would be absolutely certain that the children were dead or in terrible trouble somewhere. Whatever the worst-case scenario was, one of them would dream it up and receive silence from the other. None of this was helping the situation, but the more their worry stretched out and the longer the children were away for, the less they were able to fabricate any kind of hope that something good was to come.

They would share some moments by holding hands as they watched the skies, turning in all directions together to see if one of them could find just one small part of the sky that was proof of the children's work. A sliver of blue, the smallest cloud floating past; anything at all other than the same, constant, lifeless, dark skies and inky sea that seemed to mock them the longer this went on.

"I'm sorry." The shadow didn't even turn to say this, its blurred face staring straight out at the horizon. *Atum* did turn, though, because of all things to break what had been an unbearably long silence, that was probably the last he would have guessed. Usually, there was a bite to whatever they would say following a silence, mainly because the overflowing pools of guilt and pain in both of them had no outlet other than throwing barbs at the other. Thankfully, this time seemed to be quite different, so following suit, *Atum* softened himself from the battle-ready stance he was usually in.

"What are you sorry for?"

"For saying that they would be back."

"You didn't know—there's no way you could have known this would happen."

"Why not? *You* did. From the start, all the way back to when they first began exploring the boundaries, I was supportive of whatever curiosity their beautiful faces gravitated towards. What did you do?"

"I don't–"

"You *warned* me, *Atum*. You warned me, *and them*. It wasn't like this was out of the blue or a decision of whim; you said this was not a good idea. I disagreed. Now we're here. Take from that what you will."

Atum opened his mouth but couldn't think of anything to follow. With a miserable smile and a nod, his shadow let go of his hand and walked over to where they had chosen to rest—she still had the horizon in view, even while pretending to relax and not worry. *Atum* turned back to the skies with a grim look in his eyes. This is not how it was supposed to be, and what kind of power did he hold if this was not when he chose to make use of it?

"My love," He said, a sudden cold calm to his voice made her look up suddenly, concern painted clearly on her face despite the blur, "Trust me."

"What am I trusting?"

He didn't answer, instead, he turned back to the ocean with a steel-laced expression. The shadow had never seen him in such a state, and while she wanted to feel nothing but more concern, something inside told her that it would all be fine. With a very unsteady hand—probably from the torrential downpour of worry that had been building up to this apparent crescendo—the shadow raised herself to her feet and began to walk the short distance to where *Atum* was standing.

The closer she got, the more she realized that a sound she had been ignoring wasn't one of the looping ocean waves or breeze, but rather *Atum* whispering quietly under his breath. His eyes were closed as his mouth rapidly moved, what was once a whisper became absolute silence though the movements only increased in speed. Just before she was about to reach out to check on him, he began to glow.

Now, ever since the first moment that *Atum* saw his shadow, there had been a glow about him, but over the immeasurable passage of moments, it had become something that was just present rather than anything that stood out. *This* glow, though, was incandescent, causing *Atum's* shadow to throw her hands up over her face and duck down. There was something else along with the light; the shadow felt a heat radiating off of *Atum's* body as the glow became more and more intense.

She backed up even more, then finally moved behind one of the few makeshift side walls and peered over until finally the light was so violently bright that she had no choice but to look away entirely and huddle behind the wall in hopes when the overwhelming, world-filling illumination ended, the shadow would still find her partner standing there.

"My love?"

Atum's voice brought the shadow back from the hiding place she had sought to block out the violent cascade of light. The incandescent god was demanding of her whereabouts, but not in the argumentative manner in which they had been speaking to each other leading up to the glowing moment; this was *different* and came from a place of pure love, "It's alright, you can come out, but remember," he didn't lose the soft tone, but something suddenly let his shadow know that this was a serious matter as well, "Trust me. Just trust me and I promise that everything will be well; better, in fact."

"Of course," She said, standing up from behind cover and turning to walk towards him. The shadow stopped suddenly, its eyes trying to come to terms with what it had promised to trust. With an unwaveringly confident smile, *Atum* stood right where he had been; the same low-light glow around him as usual, but something was *very* different.

He was missing an eye.

Missing may not have been the correct term, but within that immediate moment, it was all that the shadow was able to compute.

There was *Atum*, same as always, but where two eyes used to be now one, only one looked back—still beautiful—and the other was a deep-set black hole that seemed to go on forever the longer you looked into it. The shadow, the true love of *Atum*, did not understand and the panic began to rise swiftly, but for some reason, the look on his face brought a very unexpected wave of calm that enveloped his shadow in its comforting energy; enough that it was able to take a few steps closer and actually find the ability to speak again.

"Where–where–"

"Where is my eye," He ended the question for his love, the smile on his face staying just as soft and affectionate as it had ever been. She nodded to the question that had just been answered on her behalf, deciding that one attempt at speech was good for now—she would try again later when more had been uncovered. Or at least she hoped she could, the thought of speech was far from what she wanted to do. Even though he had calmed her initial panic, the confusion and worry remained; in fact, they had made their way front and center, "I promised you could trust that it would be alright, and it is. Nothing is missing, nothing is gone; not my eye or the children."

As he finished talking, the one eye that he still had left looked over to one side, the shadow's gaze following in that direction until it fell upon something beyond unexpected. Up to that point, the thought of the two of them being anything but kind to each other was unheard of, but the children being gone longer than even the shadow expected turned that on its head. Then that was upped by the sight of *Atum* glowing brighter than anything she had ever witnessed, but then that too was bested by *Atum* standing without a care in the world yet missing an eye.

The shadow was sure—absolutely definitive beyond a shadow of a doubt—that nothing could take her by surprise more than that image of the endless, imploding black hole where an eye had once called home;

she was about to be proven wrong for another consecutive time, but this was something of a different nature.

There, beside *Atum* floating mid-air, was his other eye. Just as beautiful and piercing as it had been when it resided in its usual place, but still, the reality of what was unfolding was quite jarring. With the rapid-fire events that had just occurred, the brunt of this final one was softened a bit, but not enough for the shadow to clasp a hand over her mouth. Much to *Atum's* surprise, though, she did not start backing away again. Instead, his love began taking slow, deliberate steps towards him, or steering more towards the side that just happened to have the floating eye next to it.

With each step that the shadow took toward *Atum*, the feeling of fear dissipated, and instead, a curiosity emerged that no one could ever have predicted. When she thought about the situation, though, of all the reactions to land on, curiosity was probably one of the healthier options.

"You–" The words stuck in her throat for a moment and there was a minuscule-but-violent battle between the depth of her love for *Atum* and her knee-jerk reaction to withdraw based on the visuals around them. The reason it was such a short-lived fight is because when it came to love, nothing would ever find a way to supersede the way the shadow felt for *Atum*. With a deep breath, she gathered the effort within herself and continued both speaking and inching closer towards *Atum*, "You– you still look the same, you know?"

"Really? Not even a little different." Somehow, the sparkle in that singular eye outdid the glee that his two had been able to convey. In all honesty, she had expected there to be at least a tinge of jealousy considering that she had been unable to lift him from the doldrums, and yet now he was renewed with the inner confidence and assurance of self that had resided deep inside *Atum* proudly displayed on the surface. Still, just by looking at him, she knew that for all the outward strength that she witnessed, not a single thing had changed about the character and core that made *Atum* the being she fell in love with from beneath the stone so long ago. This was not a changed man that was before her; this was simply *Atum* as he was always meant to be, realizing his full potential.

"Well," She laughed, hearing the hint of a giggle for the first time in ages, and a huge grin swept over her blurry face, "Maybe one or two things, probably just *one* though."

"You don't say? I'll have to keep an eye out for that, then," The shadow's face turned blank—which is even more impactful when your features are the product of a silhouette behind the scenes—as *Atum* smiled with the tone of someone waiting for a response they obviously expected ahead of time. It *was* funny, but she did not want to forfeit the win and so with everything she had, the shadow kept a stoic expression as *Atum's* eyebrows danced about inquisitively, "No? Not even a little break in the wall there? *An eye out?* Not a–nothing? Impressive."

"Thanks," The words were barely formed considering they squeezed through tight lips that were doing everything possible to avoid laughing. That lasted for another two seconds and then the sound of the shadow's laughter rang across every surface and over the bleak waves of *Nun*.

"Do you think that laugh will reach them?"

"I do, my love," She answered sweetly, leaning against his shoulder. There was something hauntingly beautiful and captivating about the way the far-reaching light gleamed in all directions and clashed with the usual blackness of almost everything else. Unseen crags and notches in the stone and faint outlines of clouds against the commonly blank, inky sky were revealed by the illumination, even if only for a moment. It was a world unused to the transparency that light brought to it, but even deep within each rock and wave sat the realization that some kind of evolution was coming that would change how everything was and would be forever. *Nun* could feel it as the currents swirled about, drifting amongst the expansive minds that made up the seemingly endless ocean of darkness.

Atum held his shadow as they both looked out towards the horizon, much more visible now thanks to the incredible glow emanating from all about him. As gently as ever, *Atum* straightened up and turned to his love with the same loving look, but something in his gaze made her wonder if another change was around the corner.

"There is one more thing, my dear," His eyes shifted up to where his floating eye was hovering, as it still made the shadow uneasy when it did so directly beside *Atum*, "It isn't just my laugh that I want to find our children."

"You don't mean that you–"

"No, no," He pulled it close to him again, "I am not going to be leaving you ever again. There had to be a way for me to remain by your side *and* to seek the unknown fate of our children, and so I believe I have figured out a solution."

"I don't understand. How did you–" She stopped speaking immediately as the eye drifted down until it was parallel to *Atum's* head and staring directly into her eyes.

"I don't fully understand it myself, but there was a deep longing—a cry out, even—for there to be something else I could do besides pace back and forth without end. I heard nothing and assumed no answer would come, but as it turns out there is *something* listening to what my soul is saying, even more so when the words are pregnant with heartbreak. What the actual process was—what *happened* to me—I cannot say, for one moment I was wishing and the next I was descending from the air with a new, stronger, more powerful glow yet down an eye—technically.

"Sometimes questions asked from so deep within oneself require more than *just* an answer. I will not leave you, my love, but my eye shall. Where we cannot go, it shall be our literal eye and vision so that when it discovers what has befallen our beloved *Shu* and *Tefnut*, it will lead us to their whereabouts. I feel hope that they are alive and well, but I also know that each minute spent doing nothing is another chance for their lives to be snuffed from this world."

With those words *Atum* took a few steps forward, his fingers letting go of his shadow's touch before moving to where it was just him at the edge of the *ben-ben* looking towards the same horizon his children had followed. The floating eye held its place a few feet away from his face, the two matching stares before it flitted about for a moment, and then, with a speed that was incredibly surprising, it took off across the water—its mission had begun!

ℭONCLUSION

Consider this the first few bites of a meal that promises to be both nutritious and delicious! The depth and span of Egyptian mythology aren't something that can be defined in just a few tales. However, the beauty and wonder within each one hold intrigue and mystery that has hopefully lit a fire of curiosity within you.

Your world has grown large since you first opened this book; expanding with each sentence and chapter to incorporate more knowledge, culture, and maybe even some wisdom. What we all take away from these literary experiences will, of course, vary from one person to another, but what is shared during the time within that magic can be appreciated and related to by all of us.

As you move forward through the next days, weeks, and years of your life, consider the interest that was piqued by the lives you learned about and the worlds that opened themselves to you. Carrying that into whatever comes next is what was always intended by those who first started to pass the amazing stories on for generations ahead to learn from.

The hope is that you enjoyed this journey, but if you gained something of true value, then it is all the more perfect of a parallel to the myths that sparked it. Never stop learning, growing, or discovering; the myths will always be there, waiting, all we need to do is let them in.

www.ingramcontent.com/pod-product-compliance
Lightning Source LLC
Chambersburg PA
CBHW040235170726
48295CB00014B/924